Santa's Boots

A.P. Cooper

layout & design A.P. Cooper

Copyright 2021 A.P. Cooper

www.apcooper.net

ISBN 978-1-7399849-0-8

"I deliver the presents in one night, its quite hard work, and by the time I've finished I'm very very tired."

Santa cleans his teeth and gets ready for bed

"I wake up early on **Christmas Eve** and my Elves have made all the presents, ready for me to deliver."

Meoww!

"Then I get dressed."

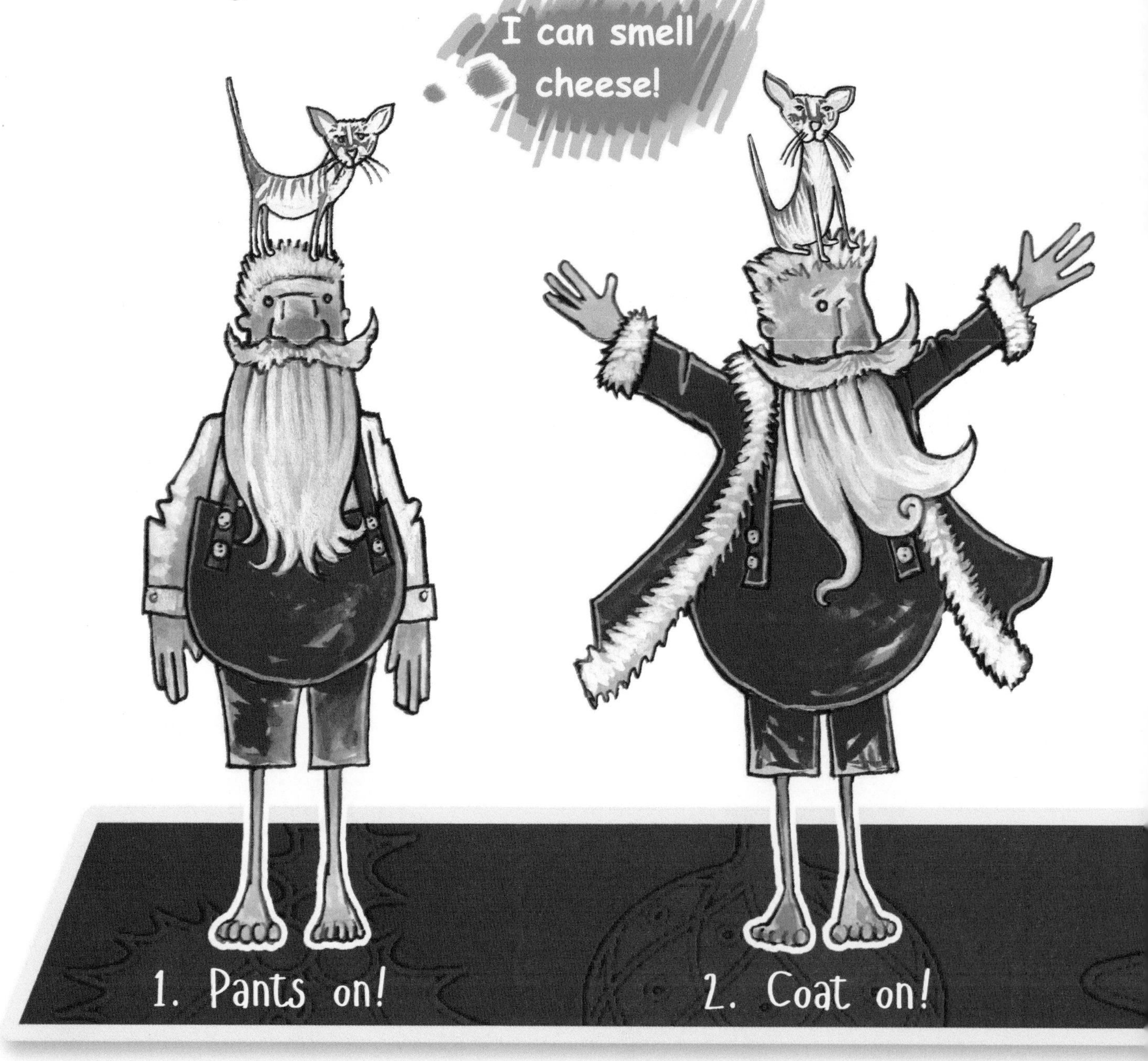

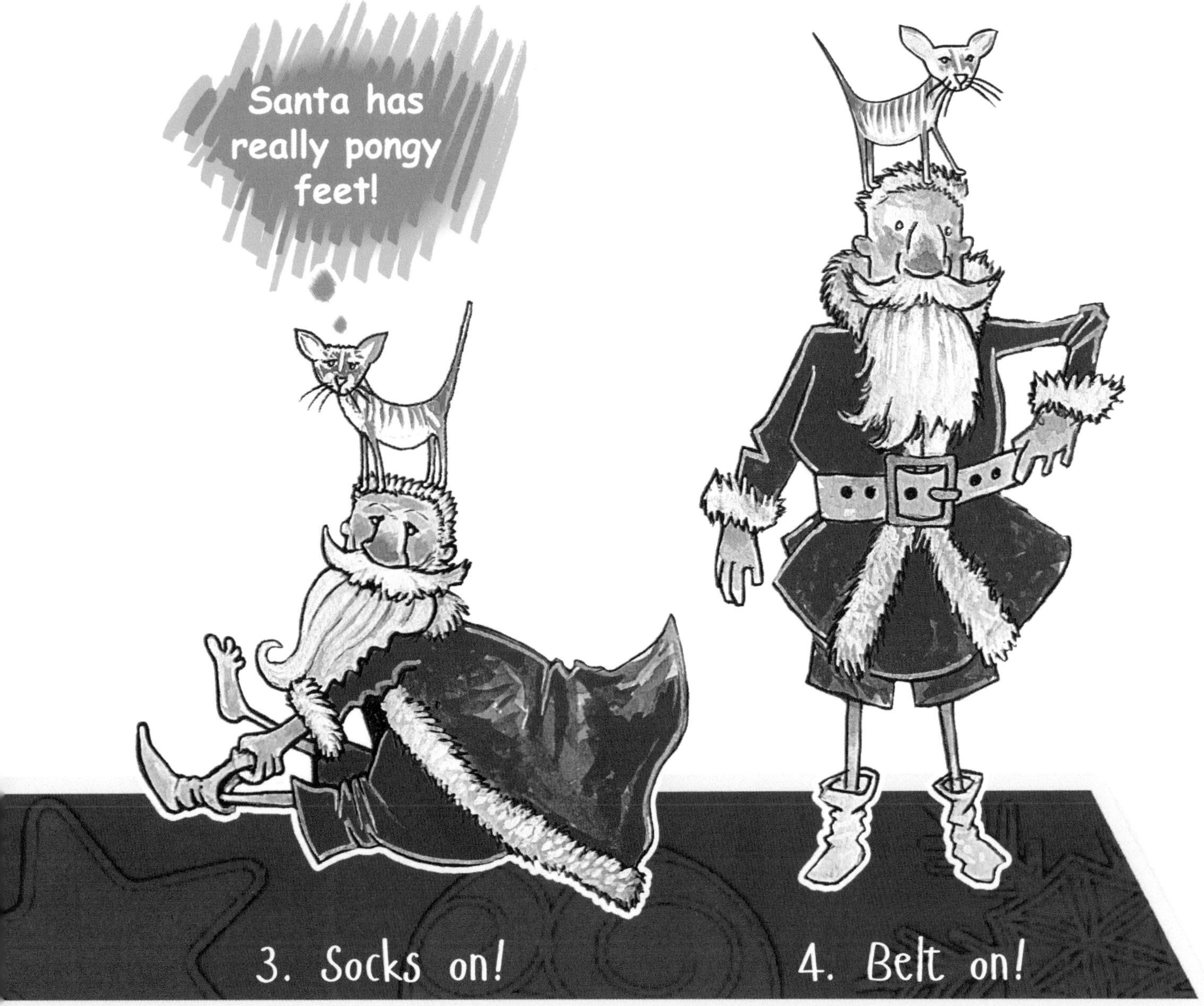
Santa has really pongy feet!
3. Socks on!
4. Belt on!

They tried everything they could think of

"Elves this will not work!
Find my **Magic Boots**" said Santa who
was getting a little cross.

The Elves looked everywhere but they could not find Santa's Boots

They brought Santa all the boots and shoes they could find.
"Try these on Santa" cried the Elves.

Santa tried
roller skates

Santa tried
Rock Star
Boots

TWANG TWANG TWANG TWANG
TWANG TWANG TWANG TWANG TWANG
TWANG TWANG TWANG TWANG
TWANG

TWANG

Finally Santa tried Explorer Boots

Oooh!

"These boots are nice and comfy."

We followed the boot prints

"With the help of my new friend, Mr Boots the Polar Bear, and my Magic Boots, we managed to deliver all the Christmas presents to every child in the whole wide world!"

THE END

Printed in Great Britain
by Amazon

14640233R00018